I0608283

SEDUCING SOMA

GALACTIC FEDERATION SERIES –

BOOK II
THE RETRIEVER SERIES

C. A. SALO

Other Works by C. A. Salo

<u>UNDERCOVER LOVER SERIES</u>

ZACK

GABE

JAKE

MITCH - Prequel

Being part of a special police unit, love was the last emotion these four brothers thought they would have to deal with.

Until they ran into the women who yanked their heartstrings.

GALACTIC FEDERATION SERIES:

Sub-series: RETREIVERS

JANESKA – Book 1

Youngest of her Retriever team, she's also the most naïve and less aggressive of the three.

During a scouting mission gone wrong, water born, Janeska Fanovana, jumps in to save the life of an impulsive youth and comes face to face with a King of Dragons as he brings her back to the water's surface, declaring he will find her before she takes off.

Draven Ratnik, a High King of Nagarr, finds the little thief who broke into his houseboat and demands her servitude for a month from her commander.

But can he handle his emotions when their passionate love-making has them creating steam, declaring them mates in his culture?

Join me at the end of the book for a Preview of Mella – Book 3 of The Retriever sub-series, blurbs for The Undercover Lover Series and a look inside Janeska.

Happy Reading!!

C ~

CHAPTER 1

"BY THE GODS!" Mella yelled. "Do not let anything happen to her! Draven will never let her come on another mission!"

Soma growled, grunting with the strain encompassing her body, as she held the boulder over Janeska's head. "Oh, sure! Leave it all to me!" she snapped as Janeska flung the rock with a wave of water, her other hand lifted in the direction of the enemy, taking him out, but not before Soma groaned, her eyes narrowed, mouth parted on a gasp as pain flooded her senses.

"She's been shot!" Janeska yelled.

Soma fell to her knees, hand going to her side as the acid burned through her chest plate. Her hands shook as she hit the clasps, Janeska jumped in, helping to get it off as fast as they could. The shot not only sent a bullet of metal, but it had an acid attached to the front, to eat through any shielding, and when the metal bullet sank into flesh it would break apart dispersing in many pieces over the area. It was a good idea in reality, it would take down a target quicker, unless you were the target. "People need to start respecting the Retriever badge a bit more." She ground out.

"It's off, it's off." Janeska breathed. "Yeah, right, when the criminals stop stealing stuff, I am sure they will."

Soma gasped with relief as Janeska used her water abilities to wash the acid away from her skin. Unfortunately, the bullet was not only one, but a cluster. "Ah shit get ready to catch me." She groaned when it engaged shooting the bullets out into her as darkness ensued.

*

Soma smiled as she stepped up to Janeska. "Hey, I'm ready."

"Are you sure you are well enough to leave?" Janeska asked.

"Yeah, I'm all right. Mella said R and R, so, I guess that's what I'm going to do."

"Why not stay here and recoup, you know you are more than welcome."

Soma smiled as Draven walked up behind Janeska wrapping his arm around her waist. "And I appreciate the offer and everything you have done for me. But you know what they say, like fish, guests start to stink after three days."

"By the Gods, you are so full of it!"

"You know you are more than welcome to stay Soma." Draven said.

"I know, and while the idea of a sex fling with a dragon is highly intoxicating. I think I'll look for a planet where I cannot out strength the men." She smiled when his brows lifted. "Well most of them." She knew most dragons would give her run for her money but only a King like Draven would be stronger than her.

"Our cruisers are at your disposal, and you have my house seal, so any planet especially allies will welcome you as a visitor. Do not be afraid to use it if you want."

Lifting her bag, she held back the wince. "Thanks Draven."

"Oh, and if you are really looking for a planet where the men are as strong as your world, you may want to seek out Du'Shara."

Her gaze narrowed. "The warrior planet?"

"Yes, and they are a close ally to Nagarr."

"Thanks Draven, I think I'll do just that."

"Are you kidding?" Janeska asked. "Du'Shara has odd rules about female visitors."

"And she'll be fine under my house seal and alliance." Draven replied.

Soma chuckled when they started arguing. "Janeska, I'll be fine, and if something comes up, don't worry, my favorite brother in law will be the first person I call to bail me out."

"Just don't go breaking into houses to take showers huh."

"Or pissing someone off, because you want to get in a fight." Janeska said.

"Okay, okay, geesh the room is filled with smart asses." Soma chuckled as she hugged Janeska. "Draven take care of my sister and that nephew of mine, I'll be back." Turning she headed toward the flight center.

She loved her sisters, but there was something in her lately, something she had to work through without her sisters around. Maybe her mating cycle was at its peak, telling her it was time to take a mate and settle down. But like Janeska, she would never stop retrieving, it was in her blood, what she did. But this habit of wanting to fight lately, confused her a bit. Oh, hell if she was honest with herself, it confused her a lot.

Janeska had called her out while they were on a mission, the same assignment in fact where they had met Draven. Soma frowned. She really did not know what was going on with her. It wasn't like she could just call up her family and say, hey, is this normal. She knew what the signs were of her people wanting to take a life mate. And while she had a few of them, this intense need to show her strength was beyond her reckoning. Maybe instead of R and R, she should check herself into a medical center and have them run some tests, although she could do that right here on Nagarr by Draven's medical advisors. Growling she took her seat in the cockpit and readied the shuttle to launch.

*

Soma smiled as she leaned back onto her elbows on the grass, Du'Shara was gorgeous. Her team had worked in the Southern region once in the middle of their cold season, and still it had drawn her, much like today. The sun lowered over the water's edge, the wind blew her hair back lightly and she sighed, her lashes fluttered shut. She hadn't felt this carefree in a while. She was in pain, but she didn't care, her mind was clear and free, no worries, no struggles, no work. She could fall asleep right here and just may do that, after all Du'Shara weather in this region was beautiful right now. The cold season had gone and the warm season was right around the corner, meaning no rains, no humidity, just perfect relaxing weather.

Her eyes snapped open with movement behind her.

"Where is your mate?"

Her shoulders tightened, causing pain to ricochet through her body. "I have no mate, I am a guest on Du'Shara and registered with the authorities."

"Proof."

His voice sounded familiar, but she couldn't place him. lifting her hand, she flashed the handheld scanner toward him without turning and lowered her hand when he took it. Staring out over the water. Damn why did he have to bother her?

"You are legal."

"Yes, I explained that."

"You are not of Nagarr though, I can scent and observe that much."

"You are correct, although I'm not sure if that's a compliment or complaint."

"I suppose either way you would like to take it. How do you hold a clearance from the house of Ratnik?"

Soma sighed, she really didn't feel like speaking to anyone, she just wanted to be left alone. "Listen, I don't mean to be rude, well," she snorted. "actually, I do. If my business with King Ratnik was your business, which by the way, it is not, I would tell you. Do I know him? of course I do or else I would not have his seal or his shuttle. If you want to check with him, go right ahead. I really don't care, I only wish to be left alone."

"As you say then, if you do not wish for conversation, you can now get out of my spot."

Soma finally turned her head. "Excuse me?" and damn, he was hot and familiar. Warrior hell, he was the epitome of a warrior. Her sight came to his knees and what strong knees they were, even covered she could see the muscle beneath. Her gaze traveled up his thighs, brow lifted and kegels clenched when her eyes landed on his crotch. Oh damn. He looked as big as the warrior she had taken the other night for bed sport. Her lips parted, and she turned slightly, whipping her gaze up to his hoping to cease all temptation. Clearing her throat. "So, why can I not stay here? I am not bothering anyone or being a nuisance, I'm only sitting here." her gaze going to his thick wavy chestnut hair, worn simply, it came to his shoulders. His hooded eyes reminded her of charcoal and the scar going from his right ear down his cheek did not deter from his rugged handsomeness.

"You are on my land. I do not allow anyone on my land without permission and as you do not want to have a conversation, and do not have my permission, you can leave, no matter whose house you are under."

Soma groaned. "Fine, that's fine." Moving to her knees, her hand went to her side as she pushed off the ground with the other. "I apologize, I saw no warnings posted." Holding her hand out for her scanner, she lifted her gaze to his again when he held onto it. "Listen, I was only trying to relax." When he still held onto it, she shifted her feet. If he didn't give it back, she may have to make that call to Draven. "I am sorry I trespassed, as I said, I saw no signs posted." Damn he was big, world of warriors, no shit, what a place to rest and relax on. "I really am." Her gaze narrowed when his did.

"Are you wounded?"

Soma exhaled. "Yes." She did not want to elaborate, her chest lifted with a breath as pain shot through her torso. Breathing out through her nose, her gaze narrowed. He looked really familiar. she didn't like lying, but she didn't want him to know what really happened in case it came down to a fight, she didn't need her injuries being used against her, and frowned when he lifted the scanner again.

"Then I am surprised King Draven let you out of his house and let you leave Nagarr being wounded. I hear Nagarr has wonderful medical facilities."

Her brows arched. "They do."

"You are a Retriever."

"Yes." he shouldn't be able to get that information out of the scanner. Unless he was a high sitting council member or Chieftain, shit that's all she needed.

"You were hit by a cluster round?"

Her gaze lowered, shit. "Yes."

"Four days ago, and Draven still let you leave Nagarr?"

Fuck. Soma met his gaze when he lifted his from the scanner.

"Come with me."

"Listen, I …" when Soma stepped forward, her head swam, and she thrust her arm out to balance herself. She felt his grasp on her arm as she faltered and went down as her eyes rolled back.

*

Her eyes fluttered, nostrils flared, and body ached as she rolled. Soma's gaze focused on a wall across an unfamiliar room. It was masculine, the bed beneath her soft and firm and the covers over her keeping her warm and wanting to stay under them all day.

Rolling to her back, she flung the coverlet off her, lifted the night gown. "Damn, I hate these things." Grunting with the effort to move the material, Soma glanced down to see her bandages had been changed. Her fingers ran over the new and rolled to her side, moving her feet off the bed as she sat up slowly, her feet barely touched the floor. He must have caught and carried her to his home. Wonderful, he didn't like off worlders and now he'd probably ask for something outrageous for helping her out. Well he had mentioned she was a Retriever and wanted her to follow him. Well, what else was new. Although, she wouldn't mind going a few rounds in the sack with him. She turned her head when hinges creaked as a door opened, her hand automatically went for her gun, to find it gone. Damn. Slapping her thigh, her fingers tapping against it as an older female came in.

"Hello, it is good to see you awake. I am Ita, the house matron. How are you feeling? I changed your bandages. You should have been truthful with Zedan about your wounds."

"I did not plan on being around him that long."

"Yes, well now you are to remain abed until he returns."

"Hmm, I do not think so. If you'll gather my clothing please, I shall be on my way." Soma frowned when she smiled.

"No, I have my orders and you will be remaining here until Zedan returns."

"Listen, Ita, I am not one to be held, I have a guest pass and I have broken no laws. I have every right to leave, so go, get, my, clothing."

"You are not on Nagarr now my dear, you are on Du'Shara."

Soma growled. "I am not from Nagarr, I am not dragon. I am…"

"From Ma'alema." Zedan stated as he entered. "Your long blonde hair and purple irises give that much away

Soma glanced over and met his gaze as the mountain of a man walked closer to her. "My clothing please."

"Ita you may leave." Zedan stated.

"Make sure to bring my clothing back or I'll be running around Du'Shara naked!"

"No. You Soma Ke'ino, are on rest and relaxation and will remain in my care until you are healed enough to leave."

"I am healed enough." She snapped.

"I beg to differ. As the Chieftain of this region…"

"Oh, fuck me, really? You are Zedan Muto?"

"Yes, watch your mouth, and we've already been there. As I was saying, you are on my world, in my region, under my law. I have already informed King Ratnik of your condition, so all you need to do is lay back down and rest."

"You called Draven on me?" Soma groaned as she set her feet back on the bed, her gaze narrowed as they stayed on his. "By the Gods, I bet Janeska is loving this, I am not gone two days and they are getting called." With Draven's permission Zedan could, enforce his words to have her remain here. "I can guarantee they made a fucking bet to see how fast a call would come in. Damn it! This is pissing me off." She growled, her eyes fluttered with his smile and then felt her body relaxing and eyes closed. "No, noo, noooo." Her words slurring as darkness followed.

*

Soma woke up, her eyes blinking as she started at the ceiling. Damn warriors. Beside being incredibly strong, certain ones, like Chieftains of Du'Shara, also had the ability for mind adjustments, like making her go back to sleep and rest. Damn she hated to admit it, but he had been right, and her body needed the rest. Testing out her limbs, no pain echoed back and slowly rolled to her side, using her hand, Soma leisurely moved her leg over the edge. No dizziness, that was good. She had never been in so much pain or discomfort from getting shot, but then again, this weapon she'd never been shot with before. It was a good thing Janeska was there to put the fire out, so to say or else it could have been a lot worse.

Glancing down, she moved the cover out of the way, struggling she took the damn night gown off and flung it to the side, before looking down to see the dressings. There would be scarring from the acid, that she knew. Rising up, she moved her feet in place, making sure she had her balance and wouldn't black out on the floor. That's all she needed was another reason for him to keep her here. Stepping over she went to a room off the side her gaze landed on a pool of water. Lifting a drying cloth, she wrapped it around herself as she gazed out over the mountains. "Oh damn, now that is a sight."

"It is, and you are more than welcome to sit in the water and relax, but I am assuming you are looking for the privy or your clothing?"

Soma tensed. "Both."

"I knew it was you, the moment you spoke to me by the lake."

"So, because we had a one-night fling in the back of your cruiser, you think you are in charge of me?" There was no way she was staying in his household under his care. Turning she met his gaze. "You can see right through this can't you?"

Zedan smiled. "Yes." And chuckled when she dropped the cloth to the floor. "And I liked our one-night fling. Although I would have been gentler if I had known you were injured to the extent you are."

Soma shrugged. "Well, I liked it the way it was."

"The privy is through that door."

Soma turned, stepping into the privy to relieve her bladder. How in the hell was she going to get out of here? If she walked, she knew he would be on her and if Draven gave his agreement, there was nothing she could do about it. When she strolled back out he was waiting in the bed chamber. "You can order your med advisor to heal this now." She knew Du'Shara had the medical advance technology to do such.

"I do not want to. I like you here."

"Hoping for more sex?"

"Yes."

Her head tilted with his smile. "Well okay then, but not until you tell me why I'm really here."

"I will, after we have seen to you. Ita is having our cook make you something to eat. Until it arrives why don't you enjoy the pool. All eight moons are out tonight. I'll be back in a while."

"Very well then. Mind telling me what Draven said?"

Zedan smiled. "Nope."

Soma's gaze narrowed, as her arms crossed over her breasts. "Do you know him?"

"We've met with negotiations."

Soma followed him as he rose from the chair he had been using. "What are you not saying?"

"Your sister, Draven's mate, she is a kick. She was yelling something about not pissing you off, and you do not have the temperament to sit ideally. I am not understanding how you are related, she is a Vesi and you are from Ma'alema. Did you have the same sire?"

"No."

"Same matron?"

"No, we are not blood related."

"Hmm, well I find your blonde hair and purple irises much more pleasing to my senses."

Soma set a hand on her hip. "Are you saying my sister is ugly?"

"No, I'm saying, I am attracted to you."

Soma pursed her lips as he shut the door behind him. "Damn good thing." Turning she headed back to the readying chamber, removed her dressing and sank into the warm pool of water, her gaze on the eight moons as they made themselves known. They really were beautiful and only all eight showed once every four months. But what the hell was she going to do about Zedan? She was attracted to him, highly so, damn her nipples hardened when he said he was attracted to her and she knew they had chemistry, or else their one-nighter would not have been so pleasurable. But he did say he needed her for another reason. "Well it's either to retrieve something or he needs me to bring Draven something. Either way, work, work, work, that is all I end up doing." Sighing, she leaned back. She loved her job as a Retriever, but they needed a break every now and then. It wasn't like Mella worked them to the bone, they always had a break after each mission, especially if one of them were injured. But this was one of her inner issues and a sign she was ready to take a life mate. Sighing she lowered under the warm water, covering her breasts and wound completely.

CHAPTER 2

ZEDAN SMILED WHEN HE entered the bathing chamber, she still sat in the pool looking out over his lands and the eight moons now showing brightly. "Your meal is in the next room."

"Thank you."

"If you stay in to long, you may prune up."

Soma smiled as she met his gaze. "You think so?"

"I do." Taking a drying cloth, he held it out for her and waited until she stepped from the pool. Damn she had a sweet body. Athletic and strong, yet soft and feminine. She was shorter than the females on his planet, but just as strong, if not stronger and his cock thickened whenever he thought about her and the night they had. Patting her dry he noticed her breathing escalated. So, she was not as unaffected by him as she pretended to be.

"So, what do you need me for? Retrieving something or bringing something back to Draven?"

Zedan wrapped the cloth around her. "Perceptive."

"That is a prerequisite for my job."

Tucking the end between her breasts, he met her gaze. "I need your help retrieving an item stolen from my mother."

"Always on duty."

Zedan lowered his mouth to hers, wrapping his arm around her waist, careful of her wound. When she kissed him back, he brought her up against him. Backing off slightly, his hot breath hit her lips. "When you are healed to my satisfaction." Zedan cleared his throat as he stepped back. "I was getting ready to contact another Retriever when information came across, I had one in my region."

"And you decided to ferret me out?"

Zedan smiled. "While I was looking for you, you happened to fall right on my lap."

Soma chuckled. "Literally."

"Come, let's get you fed, and I may think about tossing a dress on you."

"Oh, geeze thanks."

"Mmmm."

"Me in a dress, this could be interesting."

"You do not like dresses?"

"It's not that I don't like them, I never have a chance to wear them. Usually I am on duty and a dress could get in my way."

"You're off duty now.

"Hmm, yes, but I still don't think it would be a smart idea."

"Why is that?" he asked as he had her sit at a small table.

Soma shrugged. "Trouble has been finding me of late and to have a dress on, knowing it could come would be, stupid."

Zedan sat across from her. Draven had imparted some information before his wife interrupted. "Trouble. What kind?"

"Fighting."

"Well that could also come from being a Retriever."

"It could."

Zedan knew she was lying, her body language and not wanting to meet his gaze gave her away. "Well, I have something to see to before I retire. If you require more, let Ita know."

"I will, thank you."

Zedan nodded as he rose and headed out of his chambers. There was something most defiantly bothering her. Draven said she was looking for fights lately, of men who may be stronger than her and that would be in line with the fight he walked into the night he met Soma.

*

"Are you sure she will help us?" Saze asked.

"Yes," Zedan replied meeting his best friend and second in commands gaze.

"And sleeping with her is?"

He shrugged. "An added bonus." Zedan had tracked her down as Soma stated. The moment her registration for his region came over. He needed a Retriever and she literally had fallen onto his lap. He had stopped at a bar for refreshment with Saze and several of his men. The Retriever had been seen in the area. He knew Soma was a female and had her stats from the registration, but he expected her to be a brunette and tan skinned, as her registration had a Nagarrian seal. He was damned surprise when he looked up to witness the fight that had broken out. A female, blonde and in Retriever gear in the center of it and kicking a fresh out the academy private's ass. The kid had landed a good hit, sending her flying back into his table and on to his lap. He smiled when she growled and jumped up heading right back in.

Zedan was surprised she lasted so long being wounded, never mind winning against the youngling. He had bought her a drink and they ended up in the back of his land cruiser having down and dirty sex. He'd loved it and hadn't cum like that since he was a youngling himself.

"Zedan, what are we going to do with her?"

"Well, I am going to fuck her while she's here healing and then she'll be off with her crew for us. I need her to retrieve mother's pendant." Breathing deeply, he met his friends gaze. "She is starting to fail without it."

"How much longer do we have?"

Zedan lowered his glass. "If it becomes necessary, I'll have Soma healed in the med chamber. But from what I've found. Her team is the best. The Galactic Federation highly recommended them."

"Is it true her commander is Mella Seiren, High Princess of Myd?"

"Yes, and that would be exiled Princess of Myd."

"From what I heard, she had every right to speak against her father."

"I as well, but you know how it goes with royalty and politics."

"Has Soma said why she was banned from Ma'alema?"

"No. I've read the reports, but you know as well as I, there is always more to the story. I spoke with Draven about Soma, but he could not give me any more insight on what had happened, especially after his mate came in and found out we were discussing her sister."

Saze grinned as he rose. "Well, at least she is attractive. Athletic, petite and breasts enough to fill a hand. Have fun my friend, but don't piss her off, she may leave without helping."

Zedan nodded his head and watched as Saze left. Downing the rest of his drink he set the glass aside and rose to find his bed.

Smiling when he entered his chambers, he found the room silent. Glancing over, he saw Soma laying on the darkened bed and moved soundlessly to his readying chamber. Undressing and stepping into the pool, he sighed, closing his eyes to the sky and moons above, until he felt a hand on his shoulder and the soft swirl of water as she straddled his lap. Opening his eyes, he met Soma's gaze. "Hello beautiful." He smiled when she did and leaned in meeting her lips, taking control when her breasts brushed against his chest, his hand lifted to the back of her head as he thrust his tongue in, he loved her moan and parted lips as he moved to her neck, kissing suckling, biting.

He grabbed her waist when she went to mount him and turned her, her back to his chest as he moved her to the edge of the pool, closer to the windows and had her grasp the rim. He came up on his knees, thrusting into her deeply as he bit the side of her neck. He knew what she needed, could feel it soaring around her, and although she hadn't picked up on the sensors yet, he would see to her needs until she was ready to voice them aloud to him.

"Oh Gods!"

Moving his hands, he gripped the edge of the pool beside hers, thrusting into her hard and fast, listening to the sounds she was making drove him crazy as her body continued to tighten around his cock.

Grunting with pleasure, he barely realized when she started thrusting back against him. "Oh yeah sweet," he rasped, the sweat beading on his hairline as he took her. "You like it hard and, fast don't you?"

Soma moaned as his thick cock rode her hard. "Yes!"

His thrust became harder and faster, her body started trembling and her kegels quivered around him, his hand went around to her nipple and pinched, urging her over the edge. His cock swelled even more, the contractions of her body clamping around him brought him to his end as he roared with the release of his seed, thrusting deep within her warmth.

Zedan collapsed against her back, rotating his hips he ended his thrusting, his hips jerked. Breathing heavily, he could hear her heart beating rapidly. "Not yet." He breathed when she moved. "I'm still coming." Moving his hips with two short thrusts, he met her lips when she turned her head. Wrapping his arm around her waist, he moved back to the seat, still buried deep within her. "Are you, all right?"

"Yes."

"Your wound?" his hand gently slid over the dressings in place.

"It's alright, a bit sore, that's what woke me up when I rolled onto my side, and I heard you in here."

"Hmmmm." Brushing his mouth against the side of her temple, he held her to him as they sat with her between his legs. His gaze lifted to the moons as they sat there. "I told you the moons were beautiful."

"They are. I have never seen such a sight before, even with all of the places we've been."

"Do you like being a Retriever?"

"I do, and I wouldn't do it with anyone but Mella and Janeska."

"How did she end up mating a King of Dragon's?"

Soma chuckled. "Well, that's kind of my fault. We had a skirmish and we won, unfortunately, I had Selma guts all over me and made her stop at a houseboat, so I could take a shower."

"Was it yours?"

"No, it was Draven's. Long story short, he came home caught us, him and Janeska hit it off and boom, she's shooting steam when she should be water shielding because she's pregnant."

"A Dragon and a Vesi, interesting."

"Oh, it has been." She chuckled. "especially when they get in a heated fight. Freaking steam everywhere. You might think you were in a sauna."

Zedan groaned when she moved her hips, grinding his semi hard cock inside her. "All right, to bed with you."

"But I want it again."

"As do I," he chuckled as he lifted her into his arms. "But until I am satisfied you are healed more, and I will not hurt you, once a day."

"Once day? Well that's just not right."

Grabbing a towel, he set her upon a stool and started drying her off. "I do not want to hinder your healing Soma." Unwrapping her wet dressings, he tended to her wound.

"I understand that, but know if I hurt, I will tell you."

Zedan met her gaze as he rose. "I would hope so. Now let's get into bed, I have a delegation meeting in the morning."

"OH, delegation, are you not the lucky one." She snorted as he carried her to bed.

Zedan chuckled as he slid behind her, bringing her back to his chest. "I feel the same sweet, I cannot stand half of the men in attendance."

"From different worlds?"

"Yes, it's a small delegation for a summit coming later this season and I was selected by our King to sit on the council."

"Again, luck you."

"You are not one for politics I take it." Cuddling her, his nostrils flared with her clean scent and picked up his musky tones from releasing inside her.

"By the Gods, no. I am the last person you want at a delegation meeting, unless it's to kick ass and take names."

Zedan smiled. "Oh, we have those as well."

"Then I will stand behind your chair and kick ass if need be. I don't deal with idiocy very well and will not put up with stupidity. It, irks me, so my mouth usually gets me in a whole lot of trouble."

"I do not want to ruin our calmness, but I read the reports on your banishment." He sensed her quickening heart beat as she held her breath. "What is missing from it?" he asked softly.

"Does it matter?"

"Yes, it matters. I would like to hear your words on the incident."

"I was banished for speaking against my commanding officer. He was going to attack an unarmed star cruiser filled with women and children, refugees from the Altarian war. I could not allow that and even though many agreed with me, they would not speak up."

"You were second in command, a high-ranking officer."

"I was, and I made my choice."

"Would you do it again?"

"Yes."

Zedan liked how she answered with no hesitation. "I am glad to hear this." Moving his arm, he cradled her breast as he closed his eyes.

"Do not use that mind shit with me again," she yawned. "Damn it Zedan."

"I am not sweet one, you are just tired, as I am."

*

Zedan grinned when he strode into the main hall to hear Soma's laugher. She had been in his home more than seven days now and today he allowed her out of his chambers. He left her in Ita's care as he left for another meeting this morning. She was healing nicely and as he would be, becoming annoyed a having to stay abed.

"Well, hey you." Soma said.

"Good afternoon sweet one, have you eaten your noon meal?" he asked as he sat at the head of the table next to Saze.

"I have and you?"

"They brought it to my study."

"Another wonderful meeting?" Saze asked.

"How I loath them." Zedan replied, his gaze on Soma as she smiled at him. "Would you like to walk with me to the lake?"

"I would."

Rising up he turned his elbow to her, smiling when she slipped her fingers into the crook. "Has Saze been keeping you entertained?"

"He has and he's pretty intelligent for your second."

"I should hope so." Guiding her out of the manor, they walked in silence, enjoying the day. "You visited at the right time of year. This season is the most beautiful."

"It is most beautiful. I've been to the Southern region for an assignment in the cold season, does your region have such weather changes as well?"

"No, we have subtle changes, some days may be hotter or cooler, but this is my favorite." Sitting down on a slight incline, he smiled when he met her gaze. "You have no doubt been on many worlds with more direct changes."

"I have." She answered.

Zedan had her sit between his thighs, his arms came around her and rested his chin on her shoulder. "Why did you get in a fight with that youngling at the bar?"

"Because he insulted me."

"How?"

"He was running his mouth on how small I was, and it was laughable to be wearing the clothing and symbols of a Retriever. So, I belted him in the mouth."

"Hmmm. Tell me Soma, is it hard being the only one on your crew who has the strength of ten men?"

She tensed. "What are you going on about?"

"I think you came to Du'Shara to prove you are still a soft woman like those you work with."

"You know nothing about me." She snapped.

He met her narrowed gaze with a smile. She was so easy to provoke. "I know you like a good fuck. I know while you may have a short temper, you have a soft side."

"If you are trying to endure me to your case, you are losing."

Zedan chuckled. "No, I am only trying to get an idea of who you are."

"All you need to know is I am a Retriever here for R and R."

"Who likes to get wild." He nibbled her ear lobe.

"Every now and then."

Zedan leaned over when her eyes fluttered to whisper in her ear. "It has been then my sweet." Nipping right behind her ear, she shivered. "We both know you are not a loose female, let your shields down Soma, so I can give you what you yearn for, what you are here searching for."

"And you know what I yearn for?"

"Dominance." He knew he was correct when she trembled. "You are in control all the time and stronger than your counterparts and the men around you. You enjoyed what we have done, you enjoy not being in control and letting me control when and how you receive your pleasure. You fought with the youngling hoping he would win, but my beautiful one, you are a strong female, even on my planet."

Soma met his gaze. "And you like it."

"I do." Brushing his lips against hers, he started slowly, making sure she was okay. "Do you want me to dominate you Soma?"

"Yes."

Lowering her to the grass, he leaned over her, a shudder crisscrossed through his body as their lips met. His tongue thrust deeply yet softly. Settling between her thighs, his hand traveled up, brushing the thin material of her dress away. His mouth lowered to tease her hard nipples as he ground his thick cock against her mound.

Her loud moan as she grabbed on to his shirt, her hips lifted, wanting.

He ground himself against her as he grasped her arms, bringing her hands above her head, his mouth lowered to hers, then to her neck, nipping, brushing the dress aside, he opened his trousers, sliding down her body, he kissed and nipped, until he came to her center heat. Spreading her with his fingers, his mouth lowered, and he licked her slowly from her anal entrance to her clit, back down and slowly dipped his tongue inside, loving the musky scent of her especially when he could scent his musk. Du'Shara warriors could smell another male's essence on a female once they mated, and one of the things that turned him on about Soma, she may love sex, but she hadn't had a male in a long time, so long, there was no male scent on her. She was picky about who she laid with. Trailing his tongue up. Zedan started working on her clit and lifted his gaze, her lips were parted, eyes closed, and breasts jiggled as she arched her back. She'd planted her feet on the soft grass and thrust her pelvis toward him. "Do not climax, Soma." He warned, his mouth back on her swollen nub and brought her right to the edge before backing off completely, smiling when she clenched her thighs together, her chest heaving as she held back her orgasm. She was used to doing what she wanted and when, well he would stop that, especially when she gave her permission for him to dominate. Zedan trailed his fingers along the sensitive flesh of her thigh and settled between them, meeting her gaze, he sheathed himself inside her with a powerful thrust.

Both groaning with the sensations of the joining and sank his teeth into her shoulder as he rode her hard.

Her cries blurred his name on her lips, his thrusts becoming harder, deeper. Every withdrawal drove her crazy, every thrust made her mad for more. He filled her beyond fullness and she cried out as he quickened his tempo.

"Do not cum until I say, do you hear me Soma?

"I, yes!"

"Tell me what you want." He growled as he nipped her bottom lip.

"I want, I want…"

The sounds of their flesh slapping together mixed with the scent of sex had her gasping for control.

"Say it!"

"I want you to…" The glide of hardness inside her, stretching her, filling her had her wanting to combust.

"Soma!"

"Let me cum! Please let me!" she cried, her nails clawing his back.

Hammering his hips between her open thighs, he growled as she withered beneath him and gave her the release she sought. His cock pounded inside her with a force he'd never experienced. "Now! Release now Soma!" his cock pulsed inside her, jerking with her cry as she flew over the edge, her kegels contracting hard and followed her, exploding inside her warmth with a roar. His body twitched as he collapsed on top of her. Their chests rising rapidly. Rolling to lay on her side, his cock still within her. "Are you, all right?"

"Oh yes. You?"

Zedan chuckled. "By the Gods Soma, I think so."

They lay there talking for a while until the sun started setting. Helping her up, he brushed the grass off her dress and away from her hair. Tucking a strand behind her ear. "I believe we shall make it on time for dinner."

"Good because I'm starving."

"Did I give you a good work out beautiful?"

"Definitely."

Zedan smiled as they entered the eating hall and seated her to his right. He hadn't had a chance to sit when his sister yelled out.

"Why is she there?"

He met Lilee's gaze as he sat. "Because I want her there."

"She's your whore not your…"

"I am no man's whore!" Soma stood staring the girl down. "I suggest you get that straight right now little girl."

"Soma, sit, you are wounded." Zedan said.

Her gaze narrowed, and the girl fidgeted. "Do, not, order me and I am fine."

His brows lifted. "Lilee, I suggest you apologize to our guest."

"She's an off worlder!" Lilee spat.

His gaze lifted as Soma's nostrils flared and noticed warriors stepping near the shadows. "She is also Ma'alema'ian and a Retriever who took down a warrior of Du'Shara. She will have no issues putting you in your place for being rude."

"Fine! I apologize for my words."

Zedan's hand touched the back of Soma's thigh, when she sat, he never lost touch and lay his palm on the top, squeezing.

"Tell your warriors to back down, if I really wanted to toss her over and smack her ass, it would have been done before they could have reached me." Soma said. Zedan's head tilted and waited until she met his gaze before he smiled, grinning when she shrugged a shoulder.

"Is she the one who is going to help us?" Lilee asked.

"Well, I guess that would depend." Zedan chuckled as he kept Soma's gaze.

"On what?"

"Is she a dense child or just spoiled?" Soma asked.

Zedan patted her thigh. "On how she is treated Lilee, so I suggest not pissing her off, she may decide to kick your ass and then leave without helping and as she is wounded, I would not wish to engage in a fight to keep her here, although, I would ask her politely to stay."

"What if I kick her ass, stay for incredible sex and then go do the job?" Soma asked.

"Do not kick it overly much, she is my little sister after all." Lifting her hand, he placed a soft kiss on her knuckles, before calling for the meal to start.

*

After the evening meal, Zedan took Soma back to his chambers, loving her again, laying with her under the warm covers, he stared out the windows at two moos hanging low. During his talk with Draven Ratnik, he had learned she may be searching for a mate. Draven had parted with the knowledge, she was itching for fights. Ma'alema females were much like Du'Shara females in that manner. When the urge for a life mate came, it made them, irritable, growly and wanting to fight. Some time's their strength would heighten until they found the warrior who could out power them. Ma'alema and Du'Shara females could not be with a male if she could out control him, mentally and especially physically. It just was not in their genetic make-up.

Sighing, he knew he was going though his mating cycle. His body wanted a life mate, his signs had been showing for a while, but he refused to take a female who could not counter him in every way, from diplomatic to the bedroom. Hell, he could spar with Soma and not worry about injuring her. Maybe he should allow his med techs to heal her, so he could see if she was the one for him, outside as well as in the bedchamber. Closing his eyes, his nostrils flare with her clean, soft feminine scent and smiled, he also liked the fact, he didn't mind laying next to her. He had never been able to sleep by a female, usually he was up and out the moment they had finished having sex. Settling his leg over her thigh, he snuggled up to her as she curled into his body and drifted off.

CHAPTER 3

SOMA LAUGHED AS THEY sparred with swords. Twirling one in her hand, she came up with another.

"Where did that come from?"

"I am full of surprises." She was in full Retriever gear. "I have weapons hidden all over me."

"And still you move as though you walk on the clouds."

Soma met his attack and smiled as they crossed swords. "That is a good thing."

"Yes, it is." He jumped back.

Soma kept her eye on him, while this was a sparring, it should still be taken seriously. She also knew several members of his household had come down to the training area and joined his warriors in the crowd. She lunged at him, striking quickly and turned recovering just as quick when he dodged, so she didn't leave herself open.

"We have been at this for an hour, are you not tired yet?" he parried.

Soma countered and attacked, her blade hitting the side of his. "Yes, but I am not one to give in."

"You cannot expect me to give in, I am a Chieftain."

"So, we are at an impasse. What the hell do we do?" stopping she lowered her blade, point to the ground and stuck it in. "I mean, I will not quit, and you will not." Shrugging her shoulders, her gaze met his as he did the same with his sword but stepped toward her.

"I suppose we stop it and pick up at a later date, no one is quitting or giving in, but I cannot continue knowing you will not stop, even with your wound and I will not be the cause of your pain."

Soma tilted her head with a smile, dropped her sword and strode to him, kissing him hungrily. Her hands cupped his face and chuckled when he growled, wrapping her legs around his waist when he lifted her. Their mouths met hungrily, and she couldn't care less who saw. His hands under her ass, he held onto her, as he thrust his pelvis against hers, his long strides quickly brought them to his bed chamber.

"You do realize, you technically gave in."

"You do realize, not giving a shit at the moment."

*

Soma turned as they stepped into his study after dinner. "So, tell me what you need me to find."

"My mother's pendant."

"Was it reported stolen with the Galactic Federation?"

"Yes, the moment she became aware of it missing."

"What details do you have?"

"Shouldn't we wait for your team?"

"If I can get information before they get here, it's better. So, spill." Soma liked how his fingers ran through the top of his head, brushing his hair back. Damn she liked how it felt when she ran her fingers through the long locks and tried to control the tremble soaring through her from wanting to.

"My mother was on a diplomacy trip, when she arrived back to her quarters, she noticed items not in the correct spot as she left them and started looking with her hand matron. The moment they found the item gone, they alerted the warriors present."

"Was this off world?"

"Yes, on Taeli."

Her gaze narrowed. "That's surprising. The Taelian government does not put up with theft in any way. Who ever it was, may have been a visitor as well." Glancing up, she saw him smiling. "What?"

"You surprise me with your knowledge."

Soma shrugged. "It is my job you know. So, tell me more about this pendant."

"The pendant is important to my mother. As her health is failing, I fear the loss is making her condition worse."

"Explain."

Zedan sighed. "Her mother gifted it to her and she needs to gift it to the female she wants me to mate with, before she leaves for the other realm."

Soma's gaze widened as she jumped back. "Whoa! Wait a minute. Are you engaged? Has she already picked someone out for you? How in the hell could you sleep with me?"

"Soma, stop. No, I am not engaged. The female as not been chosen, to my knowledge my mother gifts the pendant to who will become my mate, whether she selects her, or I do."

Her brows furrowed as she stepped back. "Are you crazy? I don't recall that being a part of your culture."

"Yes. I would have a say in it. No, it's not part of our culture, it's a family tradition. One that is important to my mother. As it was to her mother and hers before her."

Soma stood there slack jawed. "I, ah, I am a bit confused. You want me to find this pendant, so your mom can give it to another woman, even though we have been sleeping together?"

Zedan turned from her, running a hand through the top of his hair again. "I knew it was a mistake to tell you the truth. Saze told me to keep my mouth shut. The pendant is more of a family heirloom, one she wants to pass on to the female who will be my mate. I have not chosen one, although like you my mating signs are showing."

Soma blinked. "Ah, so who said my mating signs are showing?"

"Please, Ma'alem'ian mating signs are closely similar to Du'Shara's. You wanting to fight all the time, being irritable, and so forth. But if you have noticed, since we have been mating, they have subsided."

Her brows furrowed. Damn he was right. Ever since she let him take control, and dominate her during sex, her, cravings, have been lessened and she was not itching for fights.

"Ah, you know I am correct, as with mine, your signs have tapered."

"Okay, they have, but I'm confused as to why you still have sex with me, knowing hour mom is going to pick some other woman to gift the pendant to." Her gaze met his when he turned.

"As I have stated, the pendant is more of a family heirloom, a tradition, and like you, I enjoy our mating, we, are good together. You take no shit from anyone, say it the way it is and, you are not afraid to let me love you, even knowing we will get passionate."

"And your females are afraid?"

"Some are. I am a Chieftain Soma, we are known for our— dominate side and with our strength, especially during the eight moons --"

Soma grinned. "I like your dominate side and your strength." Chuckling when he reached for her, bringing her into his embrace and met his kiss. His tongue thrust inside her mouth, claiming, possessive and she moaned, her fingers threading through his hair, tugging as her legs lifted around his waist. At least he wasn't promised to another, that she could not deal with and would have had to leave.

Zedan placed her against the wall, moving her dress out of the way as her fingers tugged at the holding on his pants, grasping her buttocks and a hard-thrust set him inside her warmth.

Soma's eyes rolled as they both groaned, then squeezed his thick girth with her muscles smiling when he grunted, whimpering when he withdrew.

A screech tore from her when he plunged inside her again, her hands greedily clutching his shoulders, holding on as he became more primal, the force of his taking churned something inside her, her mind foggy with the ecstasy he created. They didn't need to speak; the incredible pleasure intensified every cell of their bodies.

The passion of their mating had her panting and he took her mouth hungrily, his hands on her hips, grinding her to him and lifting her with every lunge, moving her beyond and over the edge, crying out with her climax, her body jerked as he rammed into her faster, harder, hitting her cervix and she gasped, eyes wide. "Gods!" her head went back to the wall as her body exploded again, shattering everything inside her, her muscles contracting mercilessly around his cock as he thrust in setting himself at her core and roared with his release.

Their bodies jerked as they used the wall to hold them up, heartbeats erratic as they breathed heavily, trying for control. "By the Gods Zedan."

"If I thought it was a possibility, I would ask you to stay."

Soma's eyes popped open. "Wh-what?"

"We fit each other so perfect, if I thought you would stay, I would ask you to, but I know you have a job waiting and you are only here until you are healed."

Her hands moved along his shoulders. Would it really be so bad to take a mate? After all, Janeska had and she still worked with them, and she really liked Zedan. "But we haven't known each other very long."

"I know."

"You are like no other male I've come across and you get my juices flowing."

Zedan chuckled as he lifted his gaze to hers. "Juices flowing huh."

Soma tightened her kegels on his cock as she wrapped her arms around his neck. "Yes." Landing her mouth on his, she held on as he moved them to the divan. "And who says I could not still go out on special missions?" she met his gaze as he sat with her straddling and still embedded on him.

"Would you?"

"Not if I was with child." Moving his arms up behind his head. "Interlock your fingers and keep them there." Moving her fingertips over his bulging biceps, her mouth drooled and pussy clenched. "I have never had a multiple orgasm, I've heard of them."

"I'm full of surprises."

"But, it means something on my world."

"I know."

Soma met his gaze. "Do you think your mother or family would like the idea?"

"It's not up to them. As I have stated, it is up to me and the pendant giving is a family tradition. It is important to my mother. She will gift it to the female I choose."

"Hmmm." Could she really be thinking about mating with him? She'd been longing for something for a long time now and he had been the one to satisfy all her yearnings. Leaning forward she took his mouth, his pulsing shaft drove forward, stretching and filling her to the core. His cock jumped inside her and she moaned.

Her hands lifted to his wrists meeting his gaze as she held on to them. "That could be – interesting."

She said, gasping when he plunged into her. "Gods, you make it hard to think when you do that."

"Good." Suckling a nipple through the light material, he nipped. He moved his hands, grabbed her wrists and brought them behind her back and he thrust deeply, his grunts mixing with her groans. "You wait until I give you permission." He growled.

"I, I…."

Zedan halted all movement. It took her a moment to realize this and whimpered with want.

"You will wait until I give you permission."

"Yes, yes." He lowered his mouth to her neck and Soma groaned with every nip, her feet barely touched the floor and, rising on her tip toes she ground down against him as best she could, his hands moved to her hips as he growled at her to keep her hands behind her and lifted her hips. Soma cried out as her contracting flesh yielded to his erection, her hands landed on his knees to keep her balanced and arched her back as he plummeted inside her, taking as much of him as she could. "Zedan, please, please."

Crying, Soma begged him to let her find her release, his thumb found her clit and he pounded into her with his full power. Soma crushed herself to him, the need to be as close to him as possible as her body vibrated. "Oh, please Zedan!"

"Release for me!" he growled, meeting her gaze.

Soma kept this gaze as he plunged into her, her body convulsed, and she jerked against him, crying out with her release, her insides squeezed his cock, pelvis bucking, her lips parted as she watched the vein on his neck throb, and teeth clench as he came hard.

Soma slumped forward, her head on his shoulder, body quivering as his shaft pulsed inside her. "By the Gods."

"So, will you?"

"Will your mother let us?"

"Not until she has the pendant, but if she knows you would…"

Soma lifted her head and met his gaze. "Then ask me right."

"Soma Ke'ino, will you become my mate?"

"Yes, especially if Mella says so." She smiled at his confused look. "Don't ask why, just accept it as fact." Soma cupped his face between her hands, kissing him softly. "Are you all right with said condition?"

"Yes," he grinned. "And as she must be a sensory or telepath, you want to make sure, I have feelings for you besides the lust we've both started this with. Settle your fears my beautiful one. I do care and have feelings that have grown since we have met. I hope the same is for you."

"It is."

*

Soma ran her fingers along her side and the scar there. It was still a bit tender but that was to be expected. Sighing she moved over to the patio area gazing up at the moons still shining through the night sky. She had been here almost two months and while her relationship with Zedan had grown, his mother refused to see or speak with her. Zedan had told her not to worry, she was still recovering from a cold, but she did worry. She knew Zedan had expressed his wishes to his mother to take her as his mate, she also knew what ever his mother had said to him upset him, but he refused to tell her why. Her eyes fluttered as his arms wrapped around her from behind.

"Why are you up?"

"I had a hard time sleeping, so I figured I'd stare at the moons."

"They are beautiful, like you."

Soma sighed when he took her ear lobe between his lips. "You are such a charmer."

Zedan chuckled. "Come back to bed and stop worrying about mother."

Soma turned wrapping her arms around his neck. "Well it is upsetting that she refuses to see me, knowing we want to become mates."

"I don't know what she's going through." He sighed, drawing her into his arms. "She also knows, I do not need her permission."

"The only thing I can think of is she doesn't like me being a Retriever or that I am from Ma'alema or exiled, I mean that right there could be the biggest issue."

"I don't know Soma. Please let it bother you no more, come, let us find our bed."

Soma followed him over and cuddled up next to him as he spooned her from behind.

"How is your wound?"

"Healed. A bit tender still, but I'm healed."

"Healed enough to work?"

"Yes," she chuckled as she reached behind her to grab his cock. "and healed enough to go again."

"You my sweet can be trouble." He groaned in her ear.

Soma chuckled. "Oh, you have no idea."

*

Soma met Zedan's gaze as they sat at the table for the evening meal. She didn't want to say anything before the meal, in case he or Lilee started an argument. "I contacted my team this afternoon while you were in meetings."

"You did, and what did they say?"

"They shall be here in forty-eight hours. When they arrive, we will need to speak with your mother."

"What? No." Lilee said. "Mother is not feeling well, you know this."

"I do, and I also know in order to do our job correctly, we need to speak with her and who attended her while the item was taken."

"I do not like it, I, no, you will not speak to mother."

Soma moved her gaze from Zedan to Lilee. "I understand the worry you have for your mother Lilee, we are not looking to cause her any kind of distress, only to gather all the information she may have. If for one moment I or Mella pick up on any discomfort from Lady Juliana, we will stop."

"Okay, I guess, but you promise if she becomes tired, you will stop?"

"Mella will able to judge her health better than I, but yes, if Mella senses any discomfort by Lady Juliana, she'll know what to do."

"Mella is your boss?"

Soma smiled. "Mella is our Commander, yes." And when Lilee opened her mouth to ask another question Zedan stopped it.

"Lilee, enough, Soma and her team will in no way bring distress or harm to mother."

Soma turned to meet his gaze, her head tilted slightly, and a soft smile emerged.

"I will arrange it."

"Thank you." Her gaze lowered to his hand when he held it out to her palm up, meeting his gaze again, she grinned, set her hand upon his and followed him back to his bed chamber.

She liked being with him, and not only in the bed chamber. Soma liked it when he took time out of his day if he could to spend with her while she was healing. Whether they went for a walk, sparred with weapons or sat under a tree laughing. They matched each other well.

Meeting his gaze when he turned, she smiled softly as the door to his chambers shut. "Love me slowly."

Zedan grinned as he lowered his lips to hers.

*

Soma geared up in her standard combat uniform of dark blue pants, a short sleeve vee neck t-shirt and combat boots. The clothing was made right here on Du'Shara as they were warriors and liked sturdy, comfortable clothing, especially for battle. Weaponing up, she made sure her knives were in place as well as the gun on her right hip and the two others in a wearable holster around her back, so they lay on either side of her, below her armpits. And lastly, clipped her badge as a Galactic Federation Sanctioned Retriever on her left hip, so it showed in the front. Mella had shipped her belongings, she would have to talk to her about why, but knowing Mella, she already knew what Zedan and she had spoken about.

Grabbing her breast plate. Damn she wished she had more time with Zedan, heading out of the clothing room to the bed chamber, she tucked the ear piece in and turned it on. "Soma on line."

"Soma, good to hear your voice." Mella said. "We're in orbit now."

"Roger that." Tossing her breast plate on she caught her image in the mirror as she clicked the clasps, securing it to herself. Sighing she turned and closed her eyes. Nostrils flared, she breathed in and out slowly, readying herself, mentally changing from rest and relaxation Soma to Retriever Soma. Slapping her hands to her chest and the breast plate, she opened her eyes and headed for the door.

Stepping into the foyer, Saze and Zedan turned to her, she met Zedan's gaze.

"They're landing now. Zedan said.

Soma nodded. Hooking her thumbs on top of her gun belt, she stepped outside and walked around the side of the manor as the cruiser came in. She knew Zedan followed her and stood, hip caulked to the side as the cruiser landed. Stepping forward when Mella and Janeska emerged. "Hei, my sisters.

"Hei," Mella and Janeska said at the same time.

"Breakdown." Mella said.

"Pendant, taken while Lady Juliana was on a diplomatic mission on Taeli. Upon returning to the apartment from a diplomatic dinner, she noticed the room was not in the same condition as they left it and started looking around, her pendant was the only item taken, and Taelian security as well as the Galactic Federation were notified as soon as they noticed the theft."

"Only one item?"

"That's what the report says."

"Have you spoken to her?"

"No," her gaze lowered, then lifted again. "Lady Juliana has not been well." She stated lifting her gaze back to Mella and met the look she knew would be there, surprise. "But Zedan has made it so we may speak with her before we leave." Watching as Mella glanced behind her to Zedan.

"Interesting. Lord Muto, we will need to speak with your matron."

"Of course," Zedan said as he stepped forward. "My mother is awake and awaiting your visit."

Soma's gaze narrowed when Mella smiled. She knew, damn her, Mella knew how she felt about Zedan and had picked up on her nervous energy. How the hell she did it, Soma had not a clue, but she always knew.

Stepping behind Mella and Zedan, she followed them with Janeska by her side. Glancing over when Janeska elbowed her.

"You, all right?" Janeska smiled.

"Yeah."

Soma glanced around at the inner chambers of Lady Juliana's rooms. They were as big and opulent as Zedan's only with a more feminine touch. Stepping to the side after Zedan introduced them, she noticed Lady Juliana's gaze on her for more than a moment, until Mella told Zedan he could leave.

"I believe I shall stay." Zedan announced.

Tuning Soma met Zedan's gaze. "Zedan, let us do our job."

"There is no reason I cannot stay."

Soma noticed Mella set a hand on her hip out of the corner of her eye. "Do you trust me?"

"Yes."

She didn't realize how easily she breathed after his quick answer. "Then trust me to know, there are always reasons."

She could tell he battled internally with himself, the slight squint at the corner of his eye, the quickness in which his pupils moved.

"As you ask."

Soma leaned in when he brushed his lips across hers and set her hand on his chest, patting it as he backed up, she kept her gaze on him as he left, before turning to see Mella smiling. "Mitä hymyilet? *What are you smiling at?*"

"You my friend." Mella said.

Standing to the side, Soma let Mella do what she did and ferret out the truth. Keeping her eye on Lady Juliana, she noted the woman aged well and could see where Zedan received his skin and hair tones from. She was still a beautiful female, and her son, oh man did he do…

When Mella turned and nodded, Soma smiled, controlled her breathing and thoughts about Zedan, and thanked Lady Juliana, before following after her commander and friend.

"Hän valehtelee. *She's faking.* Yet the pendant is our mission."

Soma met her gaze, eyes wide. "Totuus? *Truth?*"

"Joo." Mella replied as she nodded. "Come, let us say good bye to your, what is he again Soma?"

Soma pursed her lips out. "I haven't said." Stopping in the hallway they all squared off. "I may, be, staying here after the mission."

"Hoot, I knew it." Janeska grinned.

"I want her to stay here." Zedan said.

Soma met his gaze as he stepped up to them.

"I have asked her to become my mate."

"Woo hoo, I knew it! Draven said there was something going on, but the smart ass refused to give me all the details, afraid I would call you or something." Janeska laughed.

"Ah shut it, you knew nothing."

"Well it is obviously something, as she couldn't keep her thoughts from turning to him as we were working."

Soma narrowed her gaze to Mella. "What do you know?"

"I am sure I have no idea what you are speaking of."

"You know damn well what I'm speaking of. What have you seen?"

Mella grinned as she met Zedan's gaze and winked. "Say good bye to your man Soma, we have a mission to complete, before we start speaking of your future."

Soma nodded as they walked a bit away and turned to Zedan. "We're off then, I'll communicate with you as soon as we have the pendant." Smiling when he took her into his embrace and lay her head on his chest.

"Not before?"

"No, no outgoing communications during a mission, unless it has to do directly with the mission."

"I'm directly connected to the mission." He grinned.

The corner of her mouth lifted. "No loop holes Chieftain Muto."

"Be safe beautiful."

"I shall do my best." Leaning into him, her lips softly touched his and sighed when he kissed her back. Stepping to the side, she smiled at him before heading after Mella and Janeska.

Once on board the cruiser, Soma leaned forward in the seat. "What did you mean, she is faking?"

"She is not as ill as she wants everyone to believe. I think she is acting being ill to hurry her son along with taking a mate."

"Well that shits. He says she cannot force him to take a mate and from what I know of Du'Shara law, he is correct, but she is also his mother."

"He's giving you what you need huh?" Janeska chuckled.

"Plus. Holy shit, I finally find a man who I cannot walk over, literally, and his mother is set to marry him off, no matter he wants to choose his own. Do you know that was the first time I have laid eyes on her since I have been there? She has refused to meet with me, see her, speak to her, all of it, even after he expressed his wish to become life mates with me." Sighing heavily, she sat back into the seat with the force of lift off. "My luck, he will go along with what his mother wants."

"Ah, but you and he did say as well as he, that he wants you to stay." Mella said.

"He asked me if I would think about becoming his mate."

"By the Gods, what did you say?" Janeska asked.

"I told him, yes. But only if Mella says so."

"How do I get dragged into this decision?" Mella asked.

"Because you have the knowledge."

Mella grinned. "I do, and he seemed pretty intent on you coming back to stay with him in the hallway."

"He is and by the Gods, I want nothing more. I have not itched for a fight since we bedded one another. Damn mating signs. Damn mothers."

"Well, I wouldn't damn his mother just yet. I think she is waiting until you return to tell you what she wants."

Soma frowned as she met Mella's gaze. "That's just stupid. Why would she wait for me to come back when I've been there for over two months recovering in the same house?"

"To see if you do come back to stay."

Her head tilted, gaze lowered to the floor and smiled as she met Mella's gaze again. "Well hot damn."

CHAPTER 4

SOMA'S GAZE SWUNG UP the outside stair case and moved slowly, weapon in front of her and knelt at the top. "You are clear." She whispered, listening to the movement behind her as Mella and Janeska moved passed her into the mansion.

They had timed the retrieval when the thief was out of his home. It turned out, he was a Taelian Lord who had been at the diplomacy meetings and had spied Lady Juliana's pendant and decided to take it for himself. What was not going to be good for him, was the fact that after every mission, they reported to the Galactic Federation and they would forward to the Taelian government who had stolen the item. The lord would not only lose his title, but all of his privileges and most likely his life. He could deny the report, but they recorded their recoveries and when the Taelian government sees, the pendant in a safe in his chambers, well, that would not bode well for him. Going up behind Janeska, she went when Mella waved them both and so on, until they reached the top of the stairs at the master's bed chamber.

"Soma clear the way." Mella whispered.

Soma walked by Janeska and Mella up to the solid wood ten-foot door and set her hand on the door handle. Lifting it, she set her other hand on the cut out and heaved it up, ripping it off the hinges and set it down on the outside as Mella and Janeska ran in to secure the room.

Going in behind them, she strode up to the wall safe, when Janeska yanked the picture covering it down. Grabbing the handle in one hand, she created a pressure balance with the other on the wall and ripped the safe door off. Tossing it as Mella reached in, taking the pendant.

"The package is secure."

Soma turned when the shuffle of feet came up behind her and pulled her weapon and shield identifying her as a retriever, as the wide eyes of a servant appeared. "We are Retrievers, your master stole, and we are claiming the item back."

When the servant nodded and left, Soma turned quickly. "Let's move!" running for the window, Mella was out as the alarm sounded and Soma shoved Janeska out as she drew up the rear.

"Shit!" Soma hissed, her back arched, teeth clenched as a volt hit her. "Go!" hobbling down the roof, she slid grabbing a pole and started down it when another volt of electricity hit her and groaned, her fingers losing their grip and cried out as she fell. Her eyes closing when a wave of water caught her, stopped her fall and lowered her feet to the ground.

Mella grabbed her and tossed her over the wall. "Can you move?"

"Yeah, yeah, I'm good." She met Mella's gaze. "Not really, let's get out of here before I fall over." Soma rose and ran with them on either side of her, she'd waiver and one of them would catch her.

Soma breathed heavily as she sat in front of the vid screen, waiting. "By the Gods, hurry up." She growled.

"I'm here," Zedan said. "Are you, all right? I haven't heard from you in four weeks."

Soma's breath caught, he was in a robe, hair messy, she must have woken him up. "Sorry, yeah, dandy, damn you look all warm and cuddly right out of bed."

"Soma, are you injured?"

Soma smirked. "Depends on how you look at it."

"Yes," Mella stated. "She is hurt, she was hit by several volts of electricity."

"By the Gods Soma, how are you even awake? Are you, all right?" Zedan asked.

Soma's eye lids fluttered, and she jerked her head. "Yeah, all good. We have the package." Her eyes rolled back in her head and she heard him yelling her name as darkness followed.

*

Soma sighed as she exited the cruiser, she had her sun shields down covering her eyes and spotted him the moment he stepped foot outside with Saze, Lilee and Ita.

"Are you well?" Zedan asked.

"Yes, I am fine. Nothing I haven't been through before." Lifting her hand, she backed up when he leaned in to kiss her and met his gaze as he frowned. Soma grabbed his arm, leading him to his study. "Listen I have spent the last four weeks trying to distance myself from you. As much as it hurts, we cannot. What if your mother doesn't give us her blessing Zedan?"

"Soma?"

His word was soft, confused, questioning and it stirred something up inside her, it tore at her insides. Her face scrunched with the want to weep. "I can't Zedan," lowering her gaze she stepped away giving him her back. "I have my pride too. I cannot kiss you knowing, if she does not give us her blessing, you will back away from me."

Zedan stepped up behind her, wrapping her in his arms. "I refuse to give you up."

Her voice cracked. "But what if…"

"What if you would have died out there, collecting the pendant for my family? What if mother does give her blessing, what if the moons descend and wipe Du'Shara out? We don't know Soma, but I do know, I want you, I want you to stay here with me, I want you as my life mate."

"I want you too." Laying her head back against his shoulder, they held each other until Saze knocked on the door.

"Sorry to bother you two, but Lady Juliana is awake and wanting to see the both of you and her pendant. Sorry, I meant to give you more time, but Lilee informed her, Soma and her team were back."

"Thank you Saze, let everyone know we shall be in attendance momentarily." Zedan said.

Soma's chest rose with a shaky breath, they moved to stand by one another and she held his hand as they walked out and down the hall.

Soma caught Mella's nod as they stepped in behind her and Zedan and stopped at the door to his mothers' suites as they were announced.

"Soma." Mella said.

When Soma turned, Mella took her free hand and pressed the pendant onto her palm. Soma met her gaze. "I don't know if I can do this."

Zedan squeezed her hand as Mella spoke. "You can, it is all good, trust me."

Soma nodded as she stepped into the room, she knew Zedan was right behind her as she strode over to Lady Juliana who sat in a chair by the windows. "Lady Juliana," unfurling her fingers she extended her hand. "We have your pendant."

"Oh!" Juliana exclaimed as she lifted the pendant. "You have, oh yes, you have. Thank you, Soma. When I had heard your team had arrived back, I almost couldn't dare to think it was true. Thank you so much, all of you."

"It was our pleasure my lady." Turning she went to leave and stopped when her hand was grabbed to see Lady Juliana holding on to her. "Lady?"

"Please, stay."

"I am not thinking that is such a good idea."

"I do. Please."

Soma backed up to the wall with Mella and Janeska as other ladies were shown into the chambers. She noticed Zedan had taken refuge with Saze on the other side as ladies filled the chamber with giggling and laughter. "It is not a good idea for me to stay. I don't know if I will be able to control myself." Stepping off to the side.

Mella grabbed her arm. "I think you'll want to, ole mum is up to more than you know."

Soma looked over when Juliana started speaking.

"The female I have chosen to gift my pendant to for the joining with my son, is in this very room. Since she has arrived at our home, she has had a noticeable effect on Zedan, and I am happy my son is thinking the same as I."

Soma lifted her gaze, and met Zedan's across the room. He was staring her down.

"Soma Ke'ino, not only did you find and bring me back my pendant, you are a female of your word. A female of loyalty and one my children cannot walk over. Come forward."

Soma's gaze widened. Was she hearing this right.

Mella shoved her forward. "That's you chickee."

Soma stumbled forward, the females parted for her until she noticed Zedan moving to his mom's side as well.

"Soma, I bless the joining of you and Zedan. I approve of his choice for mate."

She glanced down, eyes wide, she froze when Juliana held the pendant up to for her to take. "I ah,"

"She accepts." Mella hip chucked her again.

Soma caught herself from toppling onto the chair as Juliana shoved the pendant into her hand.

"She accepts!" Juliana hollered.

The room erupted into cheers as Soma stood still with the necklace and pendant dangling from her fingers.

"Are you all right?" Zedan whispered.

"I, I need air." Rushing out, Mella winked at her, lips parted she gasped as the cool air swept over her. Hands on her knees she bent down, breathing deeply. "Was that planned, did you know?"

"No," Zedan replied. "I had no idea, but your friend Mella sure knew something."

"Damn telepaths. She picked up on it and kept it from me." Breathing in through her nose and out through her mouth, she stood straight. "I don't like surprises like that. What are we going to do, are you all right with this, I mean, holy shit Zedan, I was not expecting her to give us her blessing, especially in front of all those people."

"I had a feeling she would, we've spoken since you have been gone and she kind of imparted she has been 'watching' us."

"How so?"

"Apparently, she has not been as ill as she led everyone to believe, and has been sneaking around, trying to see how we get along. She even saw us on the hill above the lake and said she turned real quick when she knew what we were up to."

"Mella said she was faking it, right before we left."

"Yeah well, she was, the little sneak."

"But I mean, are you ready for this? Ready for me? I am a Retriever, I don't know if I am ready to sit doing nothing all day, and do, lady, stuff."

Zedan growled, grabbed and kissed her hungrily. The moment she sank against him he lifted his head. "You see your reaction to me, that is why we need to be mated. You are a Retriever Soma this is fine with me, as long as you are not with child. You will be by my side, not behind me, unless it is standing behind my chair, protecting my ass at council, because I would have no other."

"But…"

"No, buts." Kissing her again.

Soma leaned into him, she loved his strength and being with him. "As long as you promise you will not try to change me."

"Never."

Releasing May 14, 2021

"This is Captain Mella Seiren of the Retriever ship Lute, why are you firing on me?"

"Mella Serien, this is Admiral Rymus Toa of the Mydian Battle cruiser Shi'a. We are seizing your ship."

Her teeth ground down. "The fuck you are! Why is a Myd ship firing on me, Admiral!"

"The High King has sent us to retrieve you."

Her fist clenched. "You can tell my, father, to go to hell! I have nothing for him!"

"We have our orders to return you to Myd, in any way possible."

… Stepping off the ramp, she listened as all work stopped as crew members turned to stare at her. Meeting their gazes, they turned quickly. Moving when the Admiral was presented. Mella met his gaze, brow lifted as she tilted her head with a smile when he walked toward her. Hmm, sexy, warrior, damn. "Your Highness."

Mella snorted. "Please, we both know I no longer hold that title."

Rymus titled his head in acknowledgment. "Captain then."

"That's fine, or Mella, now what is going on?"

"The High King has requested your return."

Mella's lips pursed as she rolled her eyes. "Yeah, what for?"

… "Listen Admiral, just tell me what the hell he wants so I can get back on my ship and get the hell away from you and your ship. Is my mother all right?"

"From my understanding, her Royal Highness is well."

Mella lifted her hand and saluted him. "That's all I need. I'm out." And headed back to her ship. Catching the slight movement off to her side.

"You are to stay on board until we reach Myd."

Mella turned to meet his gaze. "I can tell you are not of Myd, so maybe you don't know, or maybe you do, either way, I really couldn't give two shits. I am not allowed on Myd for my life time, I am an outlaw, banned, nothing more than shit my father scraped off his boot because he had a whim. So no, if my mother and brother are well, I am not, nor will I ever go back, for if I do, I just may end killing the old man as I should have done years ago and taking my rightful place. So tell me Admiral, am I under arrest?"

"No, not unless you force my hand."

Mella grinned. "I can always start shooting my way out. I am an exile after all and if you think those soldiers lurking around in the shadows will have any effect on me getting the hell out, you better think again."

Rymus sighed. "Fine, you want it straight up. Do you really think I wanted this assignment? No. I drew the short stick, why, because I am not of Myd. So just get your little ass through that door to my quarters so we can talk."

… "All right Admiral, I am in your quarters, now answer my question, what does the old man want?" Mella met his gaze when he turned.

"Your brother has been taken."

Tingles swarmed her body, fear penetrated every cell she had, her stance weakened. "What do you mean, taken?"

"His Royal Highness Prince Turi, was kidnapped while he was on an outing with his teacher."

"On an outing, where the hell were his guards, has there been a ransom demand?" she snapped.

"I have not been made aware of all the details, I was sent to retrieve you and give you the message that His majesty wants you to find the young prince and bring him home."

Mella started pacing, Turi taken, what the hell was she supposed to do, why didn't his guards stop the kidnapping, why the hell would… turning she met the Admiral's gaze. "Wait a minute now, I am a Retriever, I don't deal with negotiations or kidnappers, I do not have the skill. What is my father thinking?"

UNDERCOVER LOVER SERIES

ZACK

Shy Sydney Ripley is set up as an undercover target due to her drug using, scheming sister with sticky fingers.

When put under watch by the Special Investigation Unit, to see whether Sydney is in on the thefts occurring at the DA's office. Lead Detective Zachary Mac Cloud encompasses her into his covert world as he searches for the truth.

Torn between the feelings he's starting to feel for her and his job, Mac yearns for Sydney and the end of the case, knowing once she finds out who he is, she may not want anything more to do with him.

GABE

Two years of flirting with ADA Tamara Wong, Detective Gabriel Mac Cloud, Finally gets to work a case with the sexy and intelligent attorney.

As Tam seems more comfortable around him, Gabe starts running into her more often, giving them a chance to talk. Until he walks into what looks like a burglary gone wrong and Tamara staring at the muzzle of a revolver.

Tamara always thought of Gabe as the playboy of the station, but getting to know him showed her a different side to the strong silent Detective. When her life is threatened, Gabe's placed as her security detail and the cover story of them being in a relationship becomes real, as they get to explore each other, while finding out who is trying to kill her.

JAKE

Jakob Mac Cloud, youngest of the Mac Cloud brothers, loves to go undercover, ferret out targets and get to the truth, but had never thought, he would ever become a mark himself.

Jake has seen his brothers find happiness with the women in their lives. The walls he'd built, ripped down when Officer Catia Andres, was shot in the field, making him feel again and see what a future for them could be.

Catia Andres, a special undercover investigator, brought in to target the Mac Cloud's, their unit and the station house from an investigation started out of jealousy and hate.

Caught between duty and desire, Catia works to clear them before her secret is out, hoping Jake will want to continue their budding relationship once he learns who she really is.

MITCH – PREQUEL

Mitch is a prequel of ZACK.

Are you ready to find out what started the Mac Cloud brothers down the path to find the women they love?

Mitchell Mac Cloud, doesn't believe in fate, but after one date with Celia reed, he knows he's in trouble.

Celia, likes Mitch from the moment she meets him, and finds the Detective entirely to enticing. They like all the same things and he calm calm her with one touch, but with a psychotic boss breathing down her neck for a date, she wants to take things slow.

Until her boss sends someone to kill them.

GALACTIC FEDERATION SERIES:

Sub-series: **RETREIVERS**

A look inside …

JANESKA – Book I

Janeska shoved the goggles on top of her head as they entered the huge houseboat, and followed one of the men from the watercraft into a room. Her brow lifted. Draven sat behind a desk, his attention on the paper in front of him, ignoring her as if he didn't know she was there. Her brow lifted as his man knocked on the door before they entered, and waited for permission before they walked in. so he damn well knew she was there. Opening her hand, her bag dropped to the floor with a thud, lips pouted and her stomach flipped, as he still refused to acknowledge her presence. "Okay, so what do you want me to clean?"

"Did your head of house not explain to you what 'in my possession' meant?" Draven asked.

Her gaze narrowed. "Yeah, sure, anything you wanted. So, what, you need me to go in the water and clean this heap of junk you call a houseboat or what?"

she asked his eyes widened as he met her gaze and the male behind her laughed.

"Is this the thief?" a female asked.

Janeska turned as a female small in stature enter the study. "I am no thief. Well, if you want to get technical, I guess, I could be considered one, but then again, the real thief is not going to call the law on something they stole, which is being returned to the rightful owner, and the Galactic Federation considers being a Retriever an honorable profession." Shrugging a shoulder, she turned back to Draven "Listen, can we just get this shit started? Where are my quarters and what the hell do you want cleaned?"

Her brows lifted when he yelled over the other males' laughter for everyone to get out. Stepping to the side a bit when Draven stepped around his desk as the door shut.

"Are you being serious with me? Mella did not explain to you what I would want?"

"A bit and then Soma mentioned something about sex, but I blew that off as her ass wanting to get laid. Why? You don't want me to clean stuff or get your food or whatever?" She tilted her head with a furrowed brow as Draven slapped a hand to his forehead.

Authors Note

Thank you for taking the time to read Seducing Soma.

Mella is on the way in May and will be the last of The Retrievers sub-series.

Have no worries

The Bounty Hunter sub-series in The Galactic Federation Series, is coming next.

As always, read lots and stay spicy!

C ~

Love a book?

Help others find it by leaving a review.

Authors will love you for it!

Thanks!

Where to find me:

www.AuthorCASalo.com

FaceBook: AuthorCASalo

Google Blogger: Authorcasalo.blogspot.com

A little Bio

I have served as the Vice President of Communications and as Vice President of Programs for my former RWA chapter.

A Slave's Way Out, won The Torrid Title of the Year Award and made me a bestselling Author.

I travel between Florida and Tennessee with my family and fur baby Elvis, managing my portfolio of residential and recreational properties. I was an active manager and hold national certifications of affordable housing for over fourteen years.

Writing is my passion and I look forward to it every day!

Not so much the editing, LOL.